Farmer Green had lots of animals on his farm. Besides the cats – Molly and Tolly – and the sheepdogs – Ben and Neb – there were sheep, pigs, rabbits, hens, and one old billy goat.

The goat had a very bad temper. He snorted and shouted loudly when he was angry. Sometimes, he got so angry that he ran into things and butted them with his horns.

One morning, Farmer Green was feeding the animals in the yard. He had milk for the cats, bones for the dogs, corn for the hens, carrots for the rabbits, and a sack of oats for the goat.

"Good morning!" called Farmer Green, as he tipped the sack into the bucket in the goat's shed. The goat replied with a snort and ran to make a start on his oats. He had a big appetite, and he was very hungry.

Suddenly, a cheeky little robin swooped down and snatched up some of the oats. Then she fluttered up into an oak tree and sat down to finish up the oats.

The bad-tempered goat looked up at the robin in amazement.

“Good morning,” the little robin sang down to him. “These are very fine oats you have.”

The goat snorted angrily and stamped his hooves. Then he shook his head in disgust and bent down to have some oats.

When she had finished her oats, the cheeky little robin came down from the tree for more. She fluttered down, landing on one of the goat's horns!

This was too much for the bad-tempered goat, who got extremely angry. He ran up and down alongside the wall, snorting and stamping his hooves.

Then he stopped and looked up, expecting to see that the robin had gone. Instead, there she was, looking cheekily down at him from the oak tree.

The goat stamped his hooves, bent his head, and started to run at the tree. He was glad to see that this time the robin fled in alarm. He butted the tree trunk hard with his horns, and there was a loud CRUNCH as they smashed into it.

The tree groaned and shook, and then, with a SNAP, CRACK, CRASH, it came tumbling down on top of the goat, who found himself trapped under it.

"Help!" he cried. "Help!"

Farmer Green came running to see what all the noise was about. On seeing that the goat was stuck, he rushed to help, but the tree was too heavy for him to lift up by himself.

“I need the old red tractor!” he shouted, running off to get it. He soon drove back in it and parked it by the fallen tree. Then he ran off again to fetch a rope.

When he got back, he tied one end of the rope around the tree trunk and one end to a hook at the back of the tractor.

Farmer Green started up the tractor and used it to drag the tree along the ground, until it was off the goat completely. Then he stopped the tractor, jumped down, and ran back to have a look. The goat was free, but he did not get up.

"I think I had better call Eric, the vet," said Farmer Green.

When Eric arrived, he felt the goat's legs and ribs up and down. Then he and Farmer Green helped the goat to stand up.

The goat was feeling a bit silly, and he waited while Eric checked him one more time, without stamping, snorting, or shouting.

“The goat has been very lucky,” explained Eric. “He is a bit stunned, but he will be fine in a little while. Perhaps this will stop him being so bad-tempered next time,” he added, patting the goat on the head.

The goat, who had started to feel a bit better, looked up at Eric and snorted as grumpily as ever. Eric looked at Farmer Green and broke into a grin.

"Then again, perhaps not!" he said. Farmer Green just shook his head and smiled.